Tilly Mint
and the Dodo

Berlie Doherty

Tilly Mint
and the Dodo

Illustrated by Janna Doherty

First published in Great Britain 1988
by Methuen Children's Books Ltd
Published 1996 by Mammoth
an imprint of Reed International Books Ltd
Michelin House, 81 Fulham Road, London SW3 6RB
and Auckland, Melbourne, Singapore and Toronto

Text copyright © 1988 Berlie Doherty
Illustrations copyright © 1988 Janna Doherty

The right of Berlie Doherty and Janna Doherty to be identified as
author and illustrator of this work has been asserted by them
in accordance with the Copyright, Designs and Patents Act 1988

ISBN 0 7497 2770 5

A CIP catalogue record for this title
is available from the British Library

Printed in Great Britain
by Cox & Wyman Ltd, Reading, Berkshire

For Ann and Laurence, Holly and Rosie
and
ALL CHILDREN WHO LOVE LIVING THINGS

With thanks to Ron Rose and Barry Moorhouse, who asked me to write Tilly Mint and the Dodo as a play for Doncaster schools, and to Charlotte Allen, aged 6, for helping Janna with the illustrations.

In memory of the last dodo, which was killed
by pirates on the island of Mauritius in 1681,
and in honour of all extinct and endangered species.

Contents

ONE

A Message
from Mrs Hardcastle

It was a very windy night; the sort of night that sounds as if wild animals are roaring round the house, and pawing at the door to be let in. The sort of night that looks as if the stars are the eyes of those animals, cold and angry.

Tilly Mint couldn't sleep. She snuggled under her quilt to try and block the noise out, but still the wild animals of the wind howled at her, and still the eyes of the stars glared down at her.

'Something nice will happen,' she told herself. 'And then I'll be able to go to sleep.'

The animals of the wind laughed.

'Yes it will,' said Tilly. 'I know it will.'

The big eye of the moon winked at her as it slid away from the clouds. She could see the leaves being torn from trees, and twigs and branches too, as if they were alive and rushing for shelter. Then she saw something long and blue twisting about like an eel; wrapping itself round things and tearing itself free; dancing, as if it didn't care about the wind.

'I've seen that before,' said Tilly Mint to herself. 'I know I have.'

And then she saw something round and red, cheerful as summer, bobbing like a bubble, and she knew she'd seen that before too. She pressed her face to the window to see what else was there, and soon there came another shape, darker than the red one, and much rounder, and quite a bit bigger, and hanging on to it by a piece of string: a Mrs Hardcastle sort of shape. Tilly sat back on her heels, not daring to believe what she'd seen.

'It can't be,' she said, though she knew it was. She pulled Mr Pig out from under her pillow and held him up to have a look too.

'Look, Mr Pig,' she whispered. 'You know who that is, don't you? It's Mrs Hardcastle! Everybody said she'd gone away for ever, but I knew I'd see her again!'

But when she looked again the red thing, and the blue thing, and the darker thing, had all gone. The moon had slipped like a fox back down into the dark clouds, and the animal stars had closed their staring eyes. The wind had stopped its roaring and was just sighing gently, like someone in a deep sleep. Tilly pushed Mr Pig back under her pillow, where she knew he'd be warm, and she wriggled back under her quilt again.

'I knew something nice was going to happen,' she said.

Just as Tilly was drifting into sleep the red thing and the blue thing and the darker thing landed with a gentle bump in the middle of the woods at the end of the park that was just down the road from Tilly Mint's house. The darker thing, Mrs Hardcastle, stood up carefully. She was a bit stiff after her long flight. She tied her red balloon to an overhanging branch, and then she climbed up the tree a bit to rescue her tangled blue scarf.

'What a mess this place is in,' she said to herself, looking round. 'No animals to be seen. All the flowers squashed. Someone's been chopping trees

11

down. And all the birds are hiding! Something had better be done about all this before it's too late. I think I know just the right person to help me, too.'

Next morning there was a letter for Tilly under the milk bottle on the step. Tilly wasn't a bit surprised to see it, though her Mum was.

'Dear Tilly Mint,' the letter said. 'I'm having a little holiday in my cottage in the country. Can you bring me the box of special things I left in my attic? I've got an important job for you to do. Love, Mrs Hardcastle.'

Mrs Hardcastle used to live just up the road from Tilly Mint. She once told her she was the oldest woman in the world. There are two special things about Mrs Hardcastle that you ought to know.

She was always dropping off to sleep.

And she could make magic things happen.

All she had to do was to open her mouth, and close her eyes, and drop off to sleep, snoring very gently. And when she was asleep, all kinds of magic things used to happen to Tilly Mint. She talked to frogs, and she flew into the sky to listen to the stars singing. She hatched out of an egg, just like a baby bird. She rode on a lion's back. All kinds of things like that. And Tilly never used to talk about it much to Mrs Hardcastle, and Mrs

12

Dear Tilly Mint,
I'm having a
little holiday in
my cottage in the
country. can you bring
me the box of
special things I
left in my attic? I've
got an important job
for you to do.

Love

Mrs Hardcastle

x x x   x x x

Hardcastle never used to talk about it much to Tilly. It just happened, in the way that magic things do, and that was that.

And then, one day, Mrs Hardcastle flew away on the end of a red balloon to have adventures of her own, and Tilly Mint missed her very much. Everybody said that she'd never see Mrs Hardcastle again, but Tilly knew, in her heart of hearts, that somebody as magic as Mrs Hardcastle couldn't possibly stay away for ever.

She read her letter again and again. The strange thing was, Mum was quite sure that Tilly Mint had written the letter herself, and if you looked at it closely you could see that the writing was very like Tilly's, a bit scrawly, and a bit splodgy. You could even tell where she'd had to rub things out because she'd made spelling mistakes. But of course, as Tilly Mint pointed out, she couldn't possibly have written it herself. She'd been fast asleep all night.

'And I saw Mrs Hardcastle flying past,' she said.

Mum smiled and told her to eat up her breakfast, and Tilly slid her letter under her plate and read it every time Mum wasn't looking.

'Dear Tilly Mint, I'm having a little holiday in my cottage in the country. Can you bring me the box of special things I left in my attic? I've got an important job for you to do. Love, Mrs Hardcastle.'

'I wonder where Mrs Hardcastle's country cottage could be? And what kind of special things could Mrs Hardcastle have left in her attic? And my job! What's my important job going to be?'

All of a sudden Tilly knew that she couldn't be bothered to finish her toast, even though it was sticky with yellow marmalade that she'd helped to make. She didn't even want any more orange juice to drink. She was definitely too excited to help to clear the table.

'Can I go?' she begged. 'Please, please, Mum? Can I go round to see Captain Cloud?'

And at last Mum said yes, and Tilly Mint ran like last night's wind to the house where Mrs Hardcastle used to live, and where Captain Cloud lived now.

Tilly would never forget the day Captain Cloud had arrived in her street. He hadn't just walked along the pavement as anyone else would have done. He'd come by boat! On the rainiest day Tilly Mint had ever known Captain Cloud had rowed up the street in a little green boat and parked it outside Mrs Hardcastle's house. Tilly was the only one who'd seen him do that, but everyone knew that he was Mrs Hardcastle's brother, and that he'd come to stay. Every time it rains he brings his boat out and rows up and down the street in it, just for fun, when Tilly's the only one looking.

If you've ever seen Captain Cloud, you'll know what he looks like. His face is as brown as nutmeg, and his beard is as grey as clouds on a rainy day. He wears huge green wellies that come right up to his armpits, as if he's been poured into them, and his pockets are full of shells, and he smells of the tide when it's full of fish.

When Tilly knocked on the door, Captain Cloud was in his kitchen, singing a song about a jellyfish . . .

'Proper little squelchy things
Blobs of slime
Pink and purple bubbles
Dancers in the brine
Swirling out their skirtses
Watch them do their curtsies
Swaying in the waves like washing on the line . . .'

'Captain Cloud!' Tilly shouted through his letterbox. 'Can I come in, please?'

'Why, it's Tadpole Tilly! Pleased to see you,' Captain Cloud shouted through the other side of the letterbox. 'Come on in, little shrimp! You're just in time to hear my new song!'

'I heard it,' said Tilly. 'It was good.'

'Thank you. Very kind of you to say so. Would you like to hear it again?'

'Oh, please let me come in, Captain Cloud! I've had a message from Mrs Hardcastle, and it's important.'

16

Captain Cloud was as excited as Tilly was when he saw the letter.

'Country cottage, eh?' he said, stroking his cloud-wisp beard. 'Important job, eh? Wonder what that can be? Special things! In the attic! Well, I'll be barnacled!'

'Please Captain Cloud, can we go and look?'

Tilly ran up the stairs with Captain Cloud puffing behind her. They went right up to the very top of the house, to the dark and spidery attic where Mrs Hardcastle used to keep her most special things; the precious things that had belonged to her when she was a little girl, years and years and years ago.

'Oh, Captain Cloud,' whispered Tilly. 'Isn't it wonderful in here!'

It was a most wonderful attic, dim and quiet as a bat's cave, and draped with fluttering scarves and long birds' feathers, and piled with shells that had the sound of the sea in them, and pebbles the colour of rivers, and stones with fossils curled inside. And in the corner, lit by the dusty light from the cob-webby window, was an old basket with a piece of paper tied to the handle.

SPECIAL THINGS, the label said. CARE OF TILLY MINT.

'Captain Cloud, we've found it!' said Tilly. She pulled back the dusty headscarf that was covering the contents of the basket and peered in.

17

'There's a long black shiny thing,' she said. 'But I don't know what it is.'

'Let's have a look,' said Captain Cloud. 'Why, that's a spy-glass, Tilly-turnip-head! You look through it and you see things. You spy on things, Tilly!'

Captain Cloud crawled round the attic, spying on spiders and moths and bluebottles, while Tilly brought the other special things out of Mrs Hardcastle's basket.

'There's a yellow balloon,' she said. 'Waiting to be blown up. And a little blue feather. Haven't I seen something like this before? And there's a drawing of a funny-looking bird. I think Mrs Hardcastle must have been trying to draw a turkey, and it's gone wrong. Oh, and look, Captain Cloud. Look!'

At the bottom of the basket, wrapped up in one of Mrs Hardcastle's orange dusters, was an egg. It was as big as a yellow melon, and it was pale gold. They looked at it through the spyglass, and they polished it with the duster, and they held it up to the light of the tiny window, and, very gently, they put it back in the basket.

'What is it, Captain Cloud?' asked Tilly.

'I don't know,' he said. 'I've never seen anything like that before. Never, never, in all my travels. It looks very special to me, Tilly Mint. I'll tell you something; it looks important, but I'm blowed if I know why.'

18

He looked down at it again and scratched his cottony hair under his cap, and then he lifted up the basket and hooked it over Tilly's arm. 'If I were you I'd set off straight away with it and take it to Mrs Hardcastle.'

'That's just the trouble.' Tilly followed him down the stairs to his salty kitchen. 'I don't really know where she is. I don't know how to find her. And look, Captain Cloud. It's raining!'

He came over to the window and stood looking out at the grey drizzle splattering down the glass. He loved the rain. It was his favourite weather. He once told Tilly that when it rained anything could happen. Anything . . .

'Why, little Tilly Lobster, you don't have to let that bother you!' he said, and his voice was bubbly with excitement. 'Rain is just what you need!'

'Is it? I don't think I'll get very far in the rain, Captain Cloud.'

'I'd say rain is just right.' And he opened the door. 'Bring the basket!'

Tilly followed him down the path to the shed at the bottom of his garden. She had to duck between the raindrops, they were so fat. They slid between the cracks on the path and tumbled against each other. By the time Tilly had caught up with Captain Cloud a little river of rain was nibbling round her ankles.

'I don't like this much,' she said.

'Yes you do,' said Captain Cloud. 'Look.'

He opened up his shed door, and he and Tilly stood on the step to look in. 'Just right!' he breathed. The floor had turned into a pool of browny-green water that slapped against the wooden walls. And bobbing against the side, moored to a hosepipe, was his green boat.

'In you get, Tiddley-wink!'

Captain Cloud hauled it in and lifted Tilly and her basket onto the slippery seat.

'What's happening?' asked Tilly.

'Nothing much,' said Captain Cloud. 'Not to me, anyway. I'm going to polish my goldfish bowl today, that's what I'm going to do. But you, Tilly Fish, you are going to find Mrs Hardcastle.'

He poked his head out of the shed to look at the weather. Tilly could hear the rain gushing down the path now, like a river rushing to the sea.

'This should do it,' Captain Cloud said. 'Hold on tight as a barnacle, Tilly-my-lizard. I'm going to give you a push.'

And before Tilly knew what was happening, Captain Cloud had pushed the little boat out of the shed into the garden that was shimmering like a lake, and away she sailed; away from the shed, and away from the house, and away from all the houses in her street, and far, far away from Captain Cloud in his long green welly legs, waving and waving to her from the door of his boat shed.

21

'Bye, Skipper Mint!' he called. 'Give my love to Mrs Hardcastle!'

'Bye!' Tilly shouted back. She closed her eyes, and let herself be rocked backwards and forwards in the little bobbing boat.

'Soon,' she whispered. 'Soon, I'll see Mrs Hardcastle again.'

And, because the rocking of the boat made her very tired, she fell asleep.

TWO

The Hideaway Woods

Tilly was woken up by the sound of knocking. Her little boat was bumping gently against the roots of a tree. She lifted her basket out and then clambered up onto a reedy bank, tying the boat to a twisty root that stuck out like an elbow over the water.

There was no sign of a cottage anywhere, but when she bent down to pick up her basket she noticed a crowd of mushrooms all huddled together like little bald men at a party. They were growing in the shape of an arrow, and pointing into the woods. She followed the arrow, and there was another, and another, all gleaming in the dark undergrowth.

'I hope this is the right way,' Tilly said.

A rabbit came quietly along the path towards her.

'Is this the way to Mrs Hardcastle's?' Tilly asked it, and the rabbit turned and scampered off, flashing its tail like a torch for her to follow.

'This way! This way!' the birds in the trees sang down to her.

Tilly started to run, excited because she knew she

23

must be nearly there now. Whiskers peeped out of holes, and paws stretched out to pull back brambles for her, and there, at last, she came to the biggest tree in the woods, a huge old chestnut tree with flowers like Christmas candles on its branches, and hanging down from it was a painted sign:

WELCOME it said. MRS HARDCASTLE'S COUNTRY COTTAGE.

'Mrs Hardcastle! I'm here! I'm here!' Tilly shouted, running round the tree and looking up as if she expected to find Mrs Hardcastle sitting up in the branches with her legs dangling down. 'I'm here!'

Then she noticed a shiny brown conker hanging on a piece of string from a twig. She reached up and pulled it, and from somewhere deep inside the tree came the sound of a bell ringing. The tree creaked, and a door slowly opened. Tilly crouched down to crawl in, and found herself face to face with a badger.

'Hello!' she said. 'I've come to see Mrs Hardcastle.'

The stripes on Badger's face were white with surprise. He snuffled up to Tilly to get a better smell of her.

'Just a minute,' he grunted. He turned round and spoke anxiously into the darkness inside the tree.

'It's a person,' he muttered. 'And it wants to come in.'

'Mrs Hardcastle, it's me!' Tilly shouted over his shoulder. 'It's Tilly Mint!'

24

'Let her in, Badger!' sang out Mrs Hardcastle. 'Tilly's our special friend!'

Badger's face crumpled into smiles of welcome. He pulled open the door for Tilly to crawl in past him. And when she stood up, there was Mrs Hardcastle, smiling at her as if she'd never been away, sitting round the table having tea with her friends.

Tilly gazed about her. She didn't know where to look first.

She was standing inside a round wooden room, with just a flicker of daylight filtering through the chimney at the top. The walls of the room were knobbly, with tufts of soft green moss on them. Long curtains of trailing green and brown leaves swayed over the window holes, casting dancing speckles of sunlight and shadows.

In the middle of the tree-room was a ring of stones, with a small fire of twigs and nutshells crackling inside it, and on top of that, a kettle steaming comfortably for tea. There was a rocking chair made of bendy branches, with grass and leaves piled on it for a cushion, and a bed made of downy birds' feathers. The floor of the tree-room was sprinkled with soft pine needles that had melted down into a fine dust. The scent of these needles mingled with the sharp smell of the woodsmoke and with the rich deep breath of mushrooms and foxes and earth; Tilly breathed it in slowly, loving it.

'Mmm! Lovely!' she said.

'It is, isn't it,' agreed Mrs Hardcastle. 'Much nicer than most houses. Come and sit down and have some tea, Tilly. Come and meet my friends.'

Badger, who seemed to be a bit slow and lame, hobbled over to the table with a tree stump for Tilly to sit on.

'We're so pleased you've come at last!' he kept chuckling. 'We've been waiting and waiting.'

A small rabbit was sitting next to Mrs Hardcastle and nibbling away fiercely at a lettuce. He watched nervously as Tilly pulled up her stump and sat next to him.

'You promise you won't start chasing us or anything, will you?' he asked her.

'Now Rabbit, I told you, didn't I?' Mrs Hardcastle said. 'You can trust Tilly.'

'Don't trust anyone, that's my motto,' the rabbit said. 'Especially humans.' He said this very softly, but Mrs Hardcastle heard him all right. She frowned at him, and he sighed and tore off a lettuce leaf with his teeth and offered it to Tilly. She noticed then that he had one arm tied up in a sling.

A hedgehog with a badly bruised face lapped slowly at a saucer of milk, and its babies snuffled round it, glinting timidly up at Tilly. A mouse with both its legs bandaged up rolled some seeds across the table for Tilly to chew. They tasted quite good.

'Are they all hurt?' Tilly whispered.

Mrs Hardcastle nodded. 'I found most of them

in traps and snares, Tilly, though Hedgehog here had walked into a car. They're all a bit nervous of humans, as you can see. But I've told them all that you're coming to help, and they've been looking forward to meeting you. Haven't you?'

Her animal friends all nodded enthusiastically. Even Rabbit managed a toothy grin, after Tilly had softly stroked him between his ears.

'But what are they all doing here, Mrs Hardcastle, in this tree-house?'

'Have an apple, and I'll tell you all about them. You're in the Hideaway Woods, by the way. Some of the most special creatures in the world live here.'

She took two apples out of the pocket of her pinny and handed one to Tilly. They were the noisy sort that scrunch when you eat them, the juicy sort that trickle down your chin when you bite into them, the sort that smell so sharp and sweet that they make your throat ache to think about them.

'We've got a lot to do,' said Mrs Hardcastle, when she'd crunched through the first half of her apple. 'You've got to help me save a lot of birds and flowers and animals that are in terrible danger. Will you help me, Tilly Mint?'

Tilly sucked her apple core.

'What do you want me to do, Mrs Hardcastle?'

'I want you to listen to a very sad story, and then I want you to tell that story to every child you meet. Every single child. Will you promise me that?'

28

Tilly nodded. Above her head a family of bats were hanging upside down like a row of folded black umbrellas in their nursery roost. One of them shifted its raggedy tattered glove of a wing and peeped down at Tilly; a little mouse-face, dark and fuzzy as a bee, blinking with sleepy surprise; then it tugged its head in again and went back to sleep.

'Those are special bats,' said Mrs Hardcastle. 'They've been in terrible danger, Tilly, and there's not many of them left. But they're quite safe here, while I'm minding them.'

As Tilly watched them she felt something watching her. A creamy-backed barn owl swooped down from the high lip of the tree's opening to stare at her.

'Quite safe,' Mrs Hardcastle told her. 'You're quite safe with Tilly Mint. She's my friend, too. Now, Tilly, have you brought me the things I sent for?'

'The special things from your attic? Yes, I have.'

Tilly bent down to pick up the basket from the floor, and realised that there was an acorn-cup balanced on the edge of the stump next to hers, with a water-beetle floating in it. The water-beetle peered up at Tilly then nose-dived down out of sight. The tree-stump was hollowed out and filled with rainwater. There were two bubbles in it, and as she watched one of the bubbles winked at her, and then the other.

'They're eyes!' gasped Tilly. 'Mrs Hardcastle, there's somebody in this tree stump!'

'That's Natterjack!' Mrs Hardcastle laughed. 'Hop out, Natterjack, and say hello to Tilly.'

A small toad hopped on to the side of the stump and blinked at Tilly with its jewel eyes.

'You look a bit fed up,' said Tilly.

'You'd be fed up if you were me,' Natterjack croaked. 'I've lost my pond. I only hopped away for a couple of days, and when I went back someone had filled it up with stones and soil. All the water had gone!'

'But you're very welcome here,' Mrs Hardcastle reminded him. 'Till we find another pond for you and Beetle.'

Natterjack bulged his throat out and made a sigh that sounded like a balloon going down. 'It's not the same thing, Mrs Hardcastle. Not the same thing at all.'

He kicked his back legs out and flopped back into his tree-stump pond, till all they could see of him was the top of his head and his bubble eyes staring.

'Let's have the basket, Tilly!' Mrs Hardcastle laughed. 'What did you bring me?'

The animals at the table crowded round Tilly to see what she'd brought. The mouse with the bandaged legs managed to clamber up the side of the basket and then fell in, and lay there with his legs in the air, stuck.

30

'Serves you right for being nosey, Mouse!' Mrs Hardcastle told him, but she lifted him out gently and set him back on his tree-stump.

Tilly lifted out the spyglass first.

'My spyglass! Oh, hand it over!' Mrs Hardcastle stood up and screwed up her eye as she held the spyglass to it. 'The things I can see through here! I can keep an eye on all my animals now. I can see newts and tigers and golden eagles and brown moths! I can see backwards and forwards in time, and up mountains and down caves, and round all the corners of the world. And I can see a special island, Tilly, far away. Look!'

She handed the spyglass to Tilly, but all she could see was a fuzzy ring with something green in the middle.

'What else have you brought?' asked Mrs Hardcastle.

Tilly dipped into the basket again. 'I've brought your balloon, Mrs Hardcastle. Are we going to have a party?'

Mrs Hardcastle looked puzzled. 'Party? No, I don't think so. I can't remember why I asked you to bring the balloon now. Never mind. I'm sure it'll come in useful. Anything else?'

'A feather.'

'A feather! How strange! It's a very nice feather though, isn't it? It reminds me of a friend of mine.'

'Mr Feathers!' Now Tilly remembered where

31

she'd seen it before; at the bottom of the budgie cage that Mrs Hardcastle used to have in her kitchen.

'How is Mr Feathers, Tilly?'

'He flew away, Mrs Hardcastle. Just like you did.'

'Did he now!' Mrs Hardcastle looked surprised, and then she smiled. 'Good for him. Best thing a bird can do, to fly away. Hope he's all right though. Anything else?'

'A drawing. I think it's supposed to be a turkey, but you've got the neck all wrong. If you've got any felt pens I can show you how to get it right . . .'

Before Tilly had finished speaking, Mrs Hardcastle had snatched the drawing out of her hands. Tilly sat very still, and a bit worried, thinking that she'd hurt Mrs Hardcastle's feelings. 'Actually, it's quite a good turkey,' she said. 'I like its legs.'

'This isn't a turkey, Tilly Mint. This is a dodo. Don't you know a dodo when you see one?'

Tilly peered at the drawing. She was sure she'd never seen a bird quite like that before – very plump, with little yellow legs and a clumpy crooked beak.

'No, Mrs Hardcastle. I don't think so. What is a dodo?'

And Mrs Hardcastle sighed as if she was remembering something very sad, and said: 'Dodos are like dinosaurs. They're all dead now.' And she said it as if she was talking about some of her best friends. 'A

bit like turkeys, too. Big, fat birds. And they're a bit like you, really. They don't know how to fly. But the most important thing about them is that they've all gone, Tilly. They're all dead. No-one will ever see a dodo again. Ever.'

33

'Why, Mrs Hardcastle? Why did they all die?'

'Well, it's a long story. And it all happened a long time ago. I'll tell you later how it happened. You'll see.'

Tilly could tell that Mrs Hardcastle didn't really want to talk about it just now. 'Poor dodos,' she said.

'Yes, poor dodos. They never did anyone any harm.'

'Mrs Hardcastle,' said Tilly, after they had both sat quiet and thinking for a while. 'When you were a little girl, years and years and years ago, did you ever see a dodo?'

'I'm not going to tell you, Tilly Mint! What a question! It's over three hundred years since anyone saw a dodo! You'll be asking me if I remember the dinosaurs next! What else did you bring?'

'There wasn't anything else special,' said Tilly, looking in the basket again. 'Only this egg. It looks a bit old to me.' It looked like an ordinary egg, but yellow with age, and with a musty, dusty smell about it. 'It's not for tea, is it?'

Mrs Hardcastle lifted the egg gently out of the basket. 'My lovely egg,' she said.

'Is it very old?' asked Tilly.

'Very, very old. And very, very special. A magic egg from long ago. I keep it safe in memory . . .'

For a time the only thing that could be heard in the tree-room was the sound of the hedgehog babies snoring, and the barn owl rippling out his feathers.

'But it's no good crying over dead dodos,' said Mrs Hardcastle. 'That won't bring them back. Nothing will bring them back, Tilly. They're extinct.'

'I wish they weren't,' said Tilly. 'I wish I could see one.'

Mrs Hardcastle blew her nose and yawned. 'Oh, I'm feeling right dopey, Tilly Mint. I think it's time for my nap.'

'Is it, Mrs Hardcastle?' said Tilly, a little bit excited, and a little bit scared. You never quite knew what was going to happen when Mrs Hardcastle went to sleep.

'Just for five minutes,' Mrs Hardcastle said. She yawned again, a long, achey, sighey sort of yawn that made the spiders huddle up for comfort in their silky webs. 'By the way, Tilly. Watch out for the pirates, won't you?'

'Pirates!' said Tilly. But Mrs Hardcastle was already asleep, creaking backwards and forwards on her rocking chair, and snoring, very gently. One by one the rabbit and the hedgehogs and the badger and the mouse slipped away to their holes in the shelves and cupboards of Mrs Hardcastle's tree-house.

Tilly lay down on the bed of downy feathers. She found a blanket made of leaves stitched together, and pulled it over herself.

Everything was silent now, except for the sound of Mrs Hardcastle's rocking chair creak-creak- creaking, and after a bit that became gentler, and slower,

35

and softer, till it stopped altogether. Mice nibbled in their corners, and the barn-owl chicks fussed under their mother's wing. Deep below the tree roots a red fox stirred in his den, and licked his dam and cubs, and slipped out into the night.

Tilly turned over, rustling her leaves. She couldn't sleep. She kept thinking about what Mrs Hardcastle had told her.

Was that the special story, she wondered. Was that the story she'd come to hear?

High above her the moon slid across the deep navy-blue of the sky. It glimmered down, down, through the branches of the trees, and through the hollow chimney of Mrs Hardcastle's tree-house. It crept like pale seeping water down the twisted tree-trunk walls and across the pine-soft carpet, and when Tilly turned over again it had spilt in a silver gleam over Mrs Hardcastle's egg from long ago.

THREE

The Egg from Long Ago

Tilly couldn't make out what it was at first. The glow was as cold as a candle-flame that's just about to go out, or a moon reflected in black water. She had to find out what it was. She rustled out of her leaf-bed and tiptoed over to the glow.

'It's the egg from long ago!' she whispered.

She knelt down and touched it. 'How cold it is!' she said. 'Poor egg from long ago! How cold you are!' She picked it up in both hands. It was as smooth as a pebble. She tiptoed back to her leaf-bed and clambered in, still hugging the egg, and then she snuggled down so she and the egg were under the leaf-blanket, warm and comfortable and as soft as sleep.

And just as Tilly was drifting away on the slow tide of Mrs Hardcastle's deep breathing she heard a little tapping sound. It sounded as if someone with a tiny chisel was knocking on glass. Tchink! Tchink!

She listened, but she couldn't make it out at all.

She snuggled the egg closer to her. It was warmer now, warmer than her hands. Even under the leaves she could see that it was glowing gold. The tapping sounded again. Tink-tink-tink.

'It's not the egg, is it?' asked Tilly. And then she said, 'No, of course it isn't.'

The tapping came again.

'It is,' Tilly said. 'It's the egg. Shut up, egg. I can't sleep.' And then she heard, as tiny as if it wasn't there at all, a 'Cheep-cheep-cheep. Cheep.' Tilly put her ear closer to the egg. It was almost as hot as a stone in the sunshine. There it came again. 'Cheep,' it went. 'Cheep.'

Tilly sat up. 'It   the egg!' she shouted. 'There's a noise in the egg! Mrs Hardcastle!' But Mrs Hardcastle was fast asleep, and would never hear her now.

'I think I'm a bit scared of eggs!' said Tilly.

The golden egg began to rock gently backwards and forwards, and then faster, and faster, and Tilly felt shivers of excitement like little rivers of lightning running up and down the back of her neck. She couldn't stop looking at the egg. A tiny crack had appeared in it, like a hair. As Tilly watched the shell began to splinter out from the crack.

Tilly dived back into the leaves and buried her face in them. 'I'm not going to look!'

The cracking sound had stopped. The rocking

had stopped. The glow had gone. Everything was still and silent again. Tilly lifted up her head, and very slowly opened her eyes.

'Hello,' said a voice. 'I don't suppose you're Tilly Mint, are you?'

Tilly sat up. A large bird, a bit like a turkey, was sitting next to her, shaking bits of shell off its feathers. Its beak was twisted round in what might be taken for a smile. It had yellow legs and big feet, and it was really quite fat.

'Yes, I am,' said Tilly. 'I don't suppose you're a turkey, are you?'

'Don't be silly, Tilly!' The bird jumped down and shook its feathers out, making the leaves swirl. 'I believe turkeys are rather common birds.' She put her head to one side. 'Try again.'

Tilly took a deep breath. She hardly dared say it, even though she knew with every bone in her body what this strange bird was.

'You couldn't be a dodo, could you?'

'Yes,' said the bird. She clacked her beak with pride, and shook out her yellow wings as though she was plumping up a cushion. 'You're quite right. I'm a dodo.' She waddled about a bit, bending her legs now and again as if they were a bit stiff, and stretching out her feathers to straighten them up, like tired fingers. 'And I can't tell you how glad I am to be out at last, after all those years!'

'But you can't really be a dodo,' said Tilly. 'Mrs Hardcastle told me that dodos are extinct.'

The dodo stopped doing her exercises and stared at Tilly. 'Oh,' she said, hurt. 'Do I stink?'

'No, I don't mean that,' said Tilly, though

40

Dodo did smell a bit, she noticed. She had a funny, yolky, rotten-eggy smell about her, which wasn't surprising, really. 'Extinct means you don't exist any more.'

'Does it?' said Dodo. 'Don't I?'

'But Dodo, you *do* exist,' said Tilly. 'You're here, and I can see you, so that must mean that you exist!' And she was so excited and pleased about it all that she jumped off the leaf pile and flung her arms round her. The dodo bird squashed up like cotton wool and fluttered free, gasping for air.

'Don't do that!' she squawked. 'You'll smother me!'

'I was trying to hug you,' said Tilly. 'Because I'm so happy to see you.'

The dodo clucked deep in her throat, pleased, looking a bit pink for a bird. 'People don't usually hug dodos, Tilly,' she said shyly. 'They hunt us, and they shoot us. Or they stuff us. They eat us, usually. But they never hug us. Never.'

'They hunt you, Dodo? Why? Why would they do that?'

'I don't know,' said Dodo sadly. 'They don't really seem to like us very much. We must be very ugly birds, I suppose.'

She held out her stunted wings so Tilly could see her properly – her plump body, as grey as a pigeon; her shaggy feathers; her crooked, overgrown beak. Her stalky legs . . .

41

Tilly nodded.

'But we never did anybody any harm, you know.'

'No,' said Tilly. 'I'm sure you didn't.'

Dodo folded her wings down and put her head to one side, watching Tilly. 'They've probably eaten us all by now, you know. That's what bothers me.'

'But Dodo, I don't understand. You're still here. I can see you.' Tilly stroked the spiny feathers on Dodo's back, trying to comfort her.

'No, you don't understand, do you? I might be the only one left, you see. What's the good of being the only dodo in the world?' The dodo scrunched across the fragments of her shell, trying to sweep them up with her wing. It was as if she was trying to make an egg out of them again, so she could climb back in her shell and disappear.

She clucked unhappily. 'I don't even know where I've hatched out. I want to go home!'

'Home!' said Tilly. 'Where's that? I've no idea where home is any more. It must be very far away.'

'Over the hills and far away,' agreed Dodo sadly. 'Over the seas and through the skies. Into the wind and down the rain . . .'

'What do you mean, Dodo?' asked Tilly, puzzled.

'Back to the land of yesterday. Just to see if I

can find any more dodos. Oh, Tilly, take me home.'

'If only I could,' said Tilly. 'Back to the land of yesterday . . . because you're a bird of long ago. What a long, long way we'd have to go to get there, Dodo.'

'It's all my fault,' said the dodo. 'Don't you worry about it, please. If I could fly, it might help. But I can't, you see . . .' She lifted her stubby wings out as far as they would go and flapped them feebly. They didn't even lift her on to her toes. 'Look at that!' she said. 'I can't tell you how embarrassed I am about that, Tilly Mint. What's the good of being a bird if you can't even fly! What a mess!'

But Tilly was staring at her, trying to remember what Mrs Hardcastle had said to her . . . *'They're a bit like you, really. They don't know how to fly . . .'*

'But *I* can!' said Tilly. 'Dodo, I can! I know how to fly! Mrs Hardcastle taught me! That's what the balloon and the feather were for, in her basket of special things. But she's asleep . . ! If only I knew where she'd put them.' And she ran round in despair, looking under leaves and stones, and Dodo ran round after her, though she'd no idea what they were looking for, and at last, tired and fed up, Tilly put her hands deep into her dungaree pockets, and there they were.

'Here you are, Dodo,' she said. 'A balloon. And a feather.'

Dodo cocked her head to one side to look at them, and then she cocked her head to the other side to get a better look, and pecked at them gently, and then she said, in a disappointed voice, 'Yes, Tilly. Very nice.'

'Mrs Hardcastle gave me this special feather, long ago, and I flew to the other side of the world with it,' said Tilly. 'And one day she gave me this balloon, and she said that only people who believed in magic could fly away with this.'

'I've never even heard of magic,' Dodo said.

Tilly slowly blew up the balloon.

'It's a sort of egg,' said Dodo wistfully. She tried to peck it, but Tilly jerked it away from her just in time.

'You mustn't pop it, whatever happens, or we'll never get going. Are you ready, Dodo?'

Dodo nodded.

'Right,' said Tilly. 'You'd better have the feather, because you're the bird.' She lifted up Dodo's wing and tucked the little blue feather under her armpit. 'Don't drop it!' she warned. 'Now. Hold on to my hand.'

Dodo stretched her feathers out and placed them in Tilly's hand. Something of Tilly's excitement started to run through her, like zig-zaggings of lightning.

44

'I'm a bit scared, Tilly,' she croaked.

'No, you're not,' said Tilly. She held up her free hand, and the yellow balloon bobbed over her head on its piece of string.

'Where are we going?' asked Dodo.

'Up, I hope!' said Tilly. 'Hold tight, Dodo! It's happening!'

The string grew taut, and Tilly and Dodo both rose up, wobbling, onto the tips of their toes.

'I think I'm going to be sick!' said Dodo faintly.

'No, you're not, Dodo!' shouted Tilly. 'You're going to FLYYYYYYYYY!'

The bats opened their eyes and stared as they bobbed slowly towards them. The spiders ate up their webs in surprise and dropped down to a safer level. The barn owl in her nest turned her head right round and back again.

'A flying dodo!' squawked Dodo. 'If only my mother could see me now!'

And a sudden wind rushed down the tall chimney of Mrs Hardcastle's tree-house, swirling the swaying curtain leaves, whisking up the dusty pine needles, floating up the feathers on the downy bed, and with a huge Whooooosh! it lifted Tilly and Dodo up, up, to the very top of the tree.

And out they swung, all in a swirling rush, out above the tangle of high branches, up, up, and up, into the blue skies of the land of yesterday.

FOUR

Home Again, and Hunted

They landed almost straight away. It was a soft landing on sandy earth, and they were in brilliant sunshine. They stood up carefully, gazing round. They were surrounded by palm trees with tall scaly trunks and long-fingered palm leaves waving high above their heads.

'Hey! It's all different,' Tilly said slowly. 'This doesn't look right to me.'

'It does to me,' said Dodo happily. 'It looks just right to me. It looks just the place to find dodos.' She scurried round bushes that were vivid with deep red and purple flowers. 'Have you seen the dodos?' she clucked to the little creatures that seemed to be nestling deep in the green heart of the bushes. 'Have you seen anyone who looks like me?'

She stopped suddenly and lifted up first one wing and then the other, and peered into her armpits, and then clapped her wings across her beak. 'Oh, Tilly! I've lost it! I've dropped your feather!'

'Don't worry, Dodo.' Tilly was much too excited

about finding the far-away land of the dodos to be worried about that. 'I've still got the balloon, remember. We'll be all right.'

She tied the balloon to a knobble on the tree-trunk, where it bobbed like a reflection of the huge yellow sun. A chattering in the branches above her head startled her. She looked up to see a bird as bright as flames peering down at her.

'Look and see!' it shrieked. 'Come and see and look at this!'

More birds fluttered down to join it, and the air buzzed with the hum of their wings and flashed with the lights of their jewel colours. Monkeys swung along the branches to join them, and dangled by their long arms, jabbering to each other and pointing. A striped snake coiled itself like a spring unwinding round a log, and lay, quiet as secrets, with its quick tongue flickering.

'Well!' said Dodo. 'Look at this! Look at this, Tilly Mint! All my friends have come to meet me.'

The fire-bird floated down and circled above Dodo's head. Then it flew right up to her and pecked her on her fat cheek.

'Oi!' squawked Dodo. 'That hurt!'

The red bird flew up and up again until it had lifted itself right up over the palm trees.

'They're dodos!' it screeched. 'The dodos are back! The dodos are back!'

The cry was taken up by all the other birds, and

by the monkeys, and by the hissing snake, and by the buzzing insects and all the other little creatures in the bushes. 'The dodos are back!'

Dodo smiled her beaky smile. She darted from one bush to another, reaching up and crouching down to peck and nuzzle the creatures there.

'The dodos are back!' she sang. 'Hurray! The dodos are back!'

Tilly felt herself being nudged forward until she stood right in the middle of the dancing ring, and then one of her hands was taken by a monkey and the other by a black boar and without being able to stop herself she was lifting up her feet and dancing to the whistles of the birds.

'I'm not a dodo, you know,' she kept saying. 'I'm really Tilly Mint.' But it didn't seem to matter. They all seemed just as pleased to see her as they were to see the dodo. Dodo stood in the middle of it all and tilted back her head and crowed with joy to be home again.

But it was the fire-bird who put an end to the dancing. He'd been circling high over their heads, and his shrill alarm call froze them as if winter clouds had blotted out their sun.

'Hide away! Hide away! The hunters, the hunters, the hunters are here!'

Up the birds flew, and away the animals scampered, and all the brilliant bushes trembled into quietness again.

'Oh dear!' said Dodo. 'Where've they all gone?'

'I think they're hiding,' said Tilly.

'What a shame. I was enjoying myself then, Tilly. Weren't they nice!'

'They were very nice,' Tilly agreed. 'But I didn't see any dodos with them.'

'No, neither did I,' Dodo sighed. 'But I'm sure they'll be around somewhere.'

'But Dodo, what d'you think the fire-bird meant when he said the dodos are back?'

Dodo shrugged up her shoulder feathers. 'I don't know Tilly. Perhaps they've gone somewhere. To sleep, I should think. That'll be where they've gone. Dodos love dozing. I'll go and find them, shall I? You stay here and hide and I'll go and find all my dodo friends and bring them to see you. I know you'll like them.'

'Be careful!' Tilly begged her.

Dodo scurried away from her, too excited to listen, and calling out to anything that might happen to be within hearing distance. 'Have you seen any dodos? Have you seen anyone round here who looks like me? Quite a nice bird, tall, you know, and rather charming actually . . .'

'Caw! Caw! Caution!' A huge grey bird with yellow eyes and a hooded head swooped down and lifted Dodo up between its talons.

'Help me! I've fallen off the world!' screamed Dodo.

50

The grey bird clapped its wing across her face. 'Don't you dodos ever learn!' it hissed. 'There's danger down there. Danger!' It perched her among the fronds at the top of the palm tree.

Tilly tried to climb after them, but her arms were aching after all that flying, and she couldn't seem to lift them up high enough. She scrabbled frantically at the sides of the tree. She was alone, and the sounds of danger were growing closer.

'Hide!' the grey bird screeched.

Tilly looked round wildly. She could hear the stealthy movements of the hunter. She could just see him now as he crouched through the bushes holding a net out on a long stick in front of him. Insects throbbed round her ears.

'Dizguize yourzel,' they buzzed.

She backed into a low, sprawling bush that was heavy with hanging flowers, and bright with butterflies.

'Be zafe! Dizguize!' the insects sizzled.

'If I was a butterfly I'd be safe!' she thought. 'I know I would. No-one would harm a butterfly.'

The zizzing of the insects grew louder in her head. A hazy cloud of pale blue butterflies flittered round her. She felt the strange sensation of growing down and down till she was tiny, and light as air. Her arms stretched up over her head, and felt as if they were spreading out like fans, and lifting her up with slow beats. She was drifting up

from the ground. Air rippled round her like water . . .

A rich, heavy perfume rose up and she realised that she had landed on the silky petals of a flower, and that her beating arms had come to rest. She could just turn her head enough to see that she had wings of vivid gold with flashes and swirls of crimson, and that they were as delicate as painted silk. And she saw something else. She saw the huge pale pink face of the hunter peering down at her.

'I've never seen a butterfly like this before!' he said. 'I must have it for my collection.'

'But I'm not a butterfly!' Tilly tried to shout. 'I'm only Tilly Mint!' But her voice made no sound at all.

She flickered her wings anxiously, trying to lift herself away from the flower and the looming face. But she was too late, and too tiny. The man swung his net over her as she fluttered up. She was trapped.

FIVE

The Spell of the Lizard

'Save her! Save her!' The grey bird screamed. 'Save Dodo's friend!'

The buzzing of the insects rose to a high, angry howl, and they swarmed like a black cloud round the man and his net. He flapped his arms to try to fan them away from his face, and Tilly felt herself being buffeted about in the net, and somersaulting upside down, so that her breath bumped out of her and her wings felt bruised and shredded. Every time she managed to crawl to the top of the net she tumbled down again.

'Save her!' the bird cried.

Then the insects with stings in their tails closed round the hunter. They landed on his skin and jabbed at him angrily, so that his flesh came up in big red bumps. They fizzed round his eyes and his ears, and dive-bombed at his nose. They swarmed along the sweat-sticky edges of his shirt collar and his cuffs. And at last he dropped his net and ran for cover, his arms across his face and the black cloud buzzing round his head.

Pieces of wing like flower petals drifted down to the ground. Tilly, bruised and breathless, crawled out of the net. She'd never fly now, with broken wings. Someone could tread on her, easily.

'You had a lucky escape there.' A papery voice crackled, close to her ear.

'Hide!' the grey bird screeched again. 'More hunters! Hide!'

Tilly tried to hop up the trunk of the palm tree.

'That isn't the way to hide!' The papery voice crackled again. 'You can be seen a mile off, with all those colours.'

'I wish I could turn into Tilly again,' Tilly sighed. 'But I don't know how to.'

'Don't do that,' said the voice. 'Tillys are much too big to hide.'

'Then how can I hide?' Tilly could hear the snapping of twigs that meant that more hunters were coming.

The paper voice tickled her ear. 'Like me!' it said. 'Look like me, Tilly! That's best.'

Tilly looked round the tree in the direction of the voice, but all she could see was knobbly trunk, and scaly brown bark, and nothing at all that could speak.

'I'm sorry, but I can't see you!' she whispered back. 'I can't tell where you are!'

'That's the idea,' the voice scratched. 'Look again, on your left.'

Tilly looked. The tree seemed to slit its bark a tiny way, and something like a brown eye glinted out, and then closed up again. The crackle laughed. 'Saw me then, didn't you?'

'Yes,' said Tilly. 'I can see where you are, but I can't see what you are! You're not a talking tree, are you? A talking, winking sort of tree?'

The crackle laughed again. 'Look again, and you'd better be quick, or you'll miss me.'

Tilly looked again, just to her left, and this time she saw the tiny crack again, and the gleam of an eye, then another crack, and the gleam of another eye; a quick flick that showed a tail, and a tiny dart forward, and then stillness again, and nothing to see but tree trunk.

'I think I saw something,' she said. 'I think I saw something like a lizard, just for a second.'

'So you did,' the papery voice crinkled, disappointed. 'You must have better eyesight than I thought. Or maybe I'm getting old, Tilly. I used to be very good at disguises.'

It opened its eyes again, and very clearly was a lizard, scaly-skinned and flick-tailed, and then it closed them and turned back to tree bark.

'You do it, Tilly,' he said. 'It's the best way to hide.'

'But how did you do it?' asked Tilly.

'Ah, that's my secret. Lizards are like wizards. Didn't you know that?'

56

'No,' said Tilly, feeling weak and trembly. Her skin was growing tight and stretched. Her broken butterfly wings had floated down to the ground, and her arms were tucking up under her body. 'What's happening to me, Lizard?'

'Something wizardy,' the dry voice scratched. 'Don't even think about it. Just close your eyes, Tilly Lizard, and listen to the chant:

Lizards are like wizards,
We're as old
As magic spell.

We're flickery and tricksy
And whispery and wise
We're firelight and waterfall
And lightning in disguise

We're the keepers
Of the secrets
In holes of shell and bone

Where moles creep
Where owls sleep
In crack of tree and stone

Lizards are like wizards,
We're as old
As magic spell.

Never told
Never tell.'

57

'Quiet down there!' hissed the grey bird. 'Hunters!'

Tilly breathed in and squeezed herself flat against the tree, and now she could hear a quiet rustling in the bushes, a creak and snap of twigs as two hunters came pushing through a tangle of bushes and stopped for a rest in the shade of the very tree that she was clinging to. They leaned against it. She breathed softly, knowing that she was in disguise now; hidden, and safe.

Over their heads Dodo sat, dizzily swaying on the branch, with the grey bird's wing stuffed into her beak. 'I'd goid do fall off id a midid,' she tried to say, and was ignored.

The first of the hunters was a skinny man who looked as if he hadn't had a decent meal for months. He carried a wriggling sack slung over his shoulder, and when he stopped he let it fall roughly to the ground. A brown paw poked out of a hole in the sack, and he kicked it.

'Now then,' said the other hunter, a tall man with a nose like a hook. He carried a gun across his shoulder. 'They won't be fit for eating if you tread on them.'

'I can soon catch more, if I wants to.'

'Let's have a look at them,' said the tall man. He peered into the sack. 'What's the use of catching little things like that? I go in for the wild stuff. Big Game.' He sighed. 'Not that I've caught anything here.'

'That's because you're noisy. Never catch nothing if you're noisy. Got to go quiet, got to go creepy, got to scuttle like a leaf in the wind.'

'Ah, just you wait and see, I'll be the first to catch the dodo. Just you wait and see.'

The two men sat back with their arms folded, happily dreaming about the dodo they were going to catch. They didn't hear the little worried screech up in the branch above them, though Tilly did. She flicked an eye open quickly, and flicked it shut again.

'Will you know a dodo when you sees one, that's the thing,' said the skinny man. 'They're very rare.'

'Of course I'll know a dodo!' the tall one said. 'It's a great big, monster sort of thing, very fierce of course, with snappy teeth. And it growls. When I catch it I'm going to stuff it and hang it on my wall. Did you hear something squeak just then?'

The other man listened and shook his head. 'Not a thing. Now, if I catches the dodo, I'm going to eat it. I've heard they're ugly flappy birds, but nice and fat!'

'Listen! Another squeak! Did you hear that?' They both strained to listen.

The skinny man went on. 'And, what's more, they're very easy to catch, so I'm told. Do you know, they're so stupid, they can't even fly! Whoever heard of a bird that can't fly!'

59

They both seemed to find this very amusing, in fact they were laughing so much that they didn't even hear the third hunter arrive. Tilly could just see him if she slit her eye open. It was the butterfly collector. He was rubbing his arms and his neck where the insects had stung him.

'I can hear you, laughing about dodos,' he scowled. 'You needn't think you can catch one of them, you know.'

'Why not?'

'Because they're extinct!'

This time the squeak came loud and clear and indignant.

'DODO EGGS DON'T STINK!'

Many things happened then. The hunters all set off in different directions in search of the screech. The skinny one tripped over his bag, and a dozen little hairy creatures like guinea-pigs with long legs and silky rabbity ears scuttled out.

'My mole-rats!' He shouted. 'I've lost my dinner.'

The butterfly collector swung his net round to try and catch them as they darted in and out of all the legs. And the tall hook-nose, the great hunter of Big Game, stuck his gun up into the air and closed his eyes and fired.

Dodo fell from her tree like a stone dropping from a cliff, and landed with a thud in the bushes.

For a moment, everything was as still as sleep.

'Did you see that!' The tall hunter shouted, his voice strangled with amazement. 'I shot it! I killed it!'

'Oh no! Oh no! Dodo!' Tilly cried. She scuttled down from the tree, and realised she was scurrying on little lizardy legs. 'You've shot Dodo!' she shouted, and her voice scrunched like crackly paper, tiny and useless and mad with grief. 'Why did you shoot Dodo? She never did anyone any harm!'

She flicked her scaly tail like a whip and skittered under the feet of the three hunters as they ran to pick Dodo up. But when they looked inside the bush, she'd gone. They searched round it, and under it, and because Tilly was so small she could slide right among its roots. It was true. The dodo had gone.

'Botheration!' said the tall one. 'That was my best prize. I could have stuffed it and kept it on my mantelpiece for years and years and years.'

'I could have eaten it up. It was so fat it would have lasted me for a week,' said the thin one.

'I could have put it in a cage and sold it to a zoo,' said the collector. 'I'd have been famous then.'

'Botheration!' the Big Game hunter said again, and he held his gun up in the air and closed his eyes and fired, at anything at all, just to make a noise, he was so angry; and there came an answer-

ing bang that was even louder than his, and something floated down on a piece of string, something yellow and tattered and rubbery. The hunter looked at it in amazement.

'By Jove!' he said. 'I've shot two birds in one day.'

'Funny-looking bird to me,' said the collector. He picked it up and turned it over and over in his hand. 'Wish you hadn't killed it. It would have looked good in my collection.' He peered up at the tree. 'Wonder if it's got a nest up there?'

'Let's have a look at it,' the thin one said. He pulled its skin to make it stretch, and sniffed it. Then he sucked it and spat it out again. 'I'm not eating that.'

'Can't even stuff it,' the tall one said. 'Never mind. It was probably very dangerous. It's probably just as well I did shoot it.' He marched off, whistling, pleased with himself, with his gun slung over his shoulder, and the other two followed him with their empty sack and net slung over theirs.

When their footsteps had died away, Tilly crawled back out of the bush, slow and heavy with sadness. She squeezed her eyes shut against the sunlight and let her hot tears roll down her cheeks and onto the dusty earth.

SIX

Down Among the Mole-Rats

'I've never seen a lizard cry before.'

Tilly opened one of her eyes. A small brown monkey was crouched on all fours beside her, with its head touching the ground and turned to one side so that it could peer right into her face.

'Don't cry, Lizard,' the monkey said.

Tilly sniffed. 'I'm not a lizard really. I'm Tilly Mint.' Another tear wobbled down her lumpy face. 'That's one of the things I'm crying about.'

'Never mind.' The monkey put out a paw and gently dabbed up the tear. 'I like lizards.'

Tilly hiccupped. 'Thank you.'

The monkey lay down on one side so it could talk to Tilly more comfortably. 'What else are you crying about, Tilly Mint?'

Tilly took a deep breath. 'They've killed Dodo,' she whispered. 'And she's disappeared. And they've shot my balloon, so I can't fly home again. And I'm a lizard.'

It was all so much and so terrible that she

couldn't stop her tears coming again, and all the kind monkey could do to help was to pat her head and dab her tears away.

'I'm sure everything will be all right,' she said.

A shadow hovered over them, cold as clouds, and although Tilly couldn't lift up her head to look at it she recognised its screech.

'I saw it all. I saw the dodo fall,' the grey bird called.

'Where is she now, then?' asked the monkey. 'This Tilly Lizard is very upset about her.'

'They carried her away,' the grey bird screamed. 'Down the dark caves. Away, away.' And the shadow shifted away from them and flitted back up into the trees.

'Who did?' asked Tilly.

'The mole-rats!' The grey bird screeched, high up in the tree tops. 'Lifted her up on their backs and ran away with her. Down the dark caves.'

'The mole-rats!' said Tilly. 'They were the animals that escaped from the hunter's bag! Monkey, can you show me where the mole-rats live?'

'Of course I can, Tilly!' The monkey did a hand-stand, delighted that one of Tilly's problems at least had been solved. 'I should have thought of that! They wouldn't have wanted the hunters to chop poor old Dodo up, you see. Or stuff her. Sorry Tilly. But those people do terrible things to animals, they really do.'

'But where do the mole-rats live?'

'Here!' the monkey chuckled, dancing again. 'Here and here and here!'

And she pointed to holes under the tree roots.

Tilly scuttled to the edge of one of the holes. 'Down there? But it's dark, and deep, and cold down there. Monkey, will you come down with me?' she asked.

But the monkey swung up the nearest tree, somersaulting from branch to branch. 'Not me, Tilly Lizard!' she laughed. 'I like to play in the sunshine. Don't like dark holes, cold and creepy. Bye, Tilly Lizard! Good luck! I'm sure everything will be all right!'

And though Tilly couldn't see her any more, she could see the monkey's shadow swinging by its long arms from tree to tree.

She peered down the hole again. She could even smell the musky cool dampness.

'I don't suppose lizards like darkness much, either,' she thought, and taking a deep breath, she slid down into the black mouth of the hole.

It wasn't too bad at first. There was plenty of light filtering through to show her the way, and she could see the marks of little paws, and a scoop in the earth where something had been dragged along. But when she came to a bend in the tunnel the light stopped altogether, and she was darting along in darkness. When she came to a fork in the tunnel she nearly turned back again.

'Now which way? Which way? Which way? Way? Way?' her lizardy voice echoed.

'Who's that? Who's that? That? That? That?' A scared voice piped.

'Me,' whispered Tilly, trying to stop the echoes bouncing. 'It's only me.'

Something furry thrust up against her nose, nearly treading on her.

'Don't do that,' said Tilly. 'You'll squash me.'

The paw moved, and she felt a wet nose snuffling her.

'Ah, it's a lizard,' the voice said. 'You'll have to turn back, I'm afraid. They don't like lizards down there. Not much.'

'But I'm not a lizard,' said Tilly. 'I'm Tilly Mint really.'

'I still can't let you in. It's more than my job's worth. Only mole-rats allowed past this point.'

'And dodos?' asked Tilly hopefully.

'I believe I did see a dodo once, yes,' the mole-rat guard said. 'Bit fat for down here.'

'Was it just now that you saw her?'

'Might have been,' said the guard cautiously. 'Why d'you want to know?'

'Because she's my friend,' said Tilly. 'Was, I mean. Was my friend.' She couldn't stop her voice from wobbling.

'Now, now. Don't do that,' the mole-rat begged. 'You'll set me off, and once you've set me off you

68

never stop me. I'm that soft-hearted . . .' He wiped his nose on the furriest bit of his arm.

'Then please let me go on,' said Tilly.

'Couldn't you do something about this lizard business?' asked the mole-rat. 'They'd be very upset if I let a lizard go down there.'

It was hopeless. What Tilly would have liked more than anything would have been to turn back into Tilly Mint again, but that would have been no use at all. She'd have been well and truly stuck if that happened. She'd have to stay there for ever, or till she got very thin . . .

'It's more than my job's worth, you see,' he explained. 'I daren't let you past, and that's that.' Tilly could hear him stroking his beardy chin. 'Perhaps there's something else I could do for you? You've come all this way — it seems a shame to send you back again so soon. I could sing you a song, if you like. Would that cheer you up a bit?'

'Not very much,' Tilly sniffed. And then she had an idea. 'I mean yes,' she said. 'It would cheer me up a lot.'

'I love singing,' said the mole-rat. 'Better than eating, or digging, or going for long walks by a river. I love singing songs. What number would you like?'

'Erm –' said Tilly.

'Have song number 75,' the mole-rat suggested. 'It's my favourite.'

'All right,' said Tilly.

The mole-rat began to sing immediately, in the sweet, high, whistling tone of a choirboy, and now Tilly could see a little better she could just make him out, poised on his back legs with his front paws pressed together across his fuzzy chest, and his head held high, and his eyes closed.

> *'All things begin in darkness*
> *In shell, in nut, in hole,*
> *In seed, in spawn, in nest, in soil,*
> *We thank the makers of us all*
>
> *And so our grateful song we raise*
> *Sing out of darkness in their praise*
> *With squeaks and chirps and croaks and roars*
> *With wings and fins and paws and claws*
>
> *We thank the earth, our mother,*
> *We thank the sun, our father*
> *For giving us each other*
> *And the precious gift of life.'*

The mole-rat's voice echoed round and round the dark tunnels, sweet and clear as water tumbling over stones. And while he was singing, with his paws still pressed together and his eyes closed, Tilly crept past him, quiet as ripples, and down the main tunnel, and as she began to pick up speed she heard him change his tune to a piping,

70

jigging, skipping song that set him dancing and helped her to run as fast as her long-toed feet would take her.

She didn't stop running until she saw a glow at the end of the tunnel. At first she thought she'd run right through it, and that she'd met daylight again, but then she realised that the tunnel swung round a bend and that the glow came from thousands of little insects, all fluttering and shimmering along the tunnel walls and lighting up a large underground cavern. As she crept nearer, the glow became so brilliant that she was dazzled by it.

From far away at the guard's end of the tunnel she could hear his voice still trilling a jig, and the stamp of his feet as he danced to it in the darkness. Now as she broke through into the green and gold brilliance of the cavern, the same tune was echoing round and round. Dozens of mole-rats were dancing round to it, whirling each other shoulder high, singing away in high piping voices, leaping round in mad circles, and high above their voices another voice was squawking, loud and froggy and cheerful.

Tilly pressed herself down to peer under the skipping feet. Lying on her back in the middle of the ring, waving her legs about in time to the music, and with her feathers nearly black with dust, was Dodo.

SEVEN

Danger Everywhere

Tilly darted into the middle of the circle of dancing mole-rats. 'Dodo!' she cried.

The mole-rats froze into stillness.

Dodo did her best to sit up, though the roof of the cavern was too low for this. She tried to twist her head round and got her beak stuck. 'Did fomeone fpeak?'

'I did!' said Tilly. 'It's me, Tilly Mint! Oh, Dodo, I'm so glad you're still alive.'

'Of courfe I'm ftill alive!' said Dodo to the roof.

'I thought the hunters had shot you! They didn't hurt you, did they?'

'Didn't touch me!' said Dodo proudly, freeing her beak at last. 'To tell you the truth, Tilly, all that happened was that I went a little dizzy from being so high up, you know, and a bit excited I expect, and well, I fainted. I fell off the tree and next thing I knew I woke up lying on my back and being rushed along headfirst through the bushes, and then pushed down a hole, and then dragged along tunnels till I thought my head was going to come right off, and here I am at last . . . and Tilly, these dear friends did it all, and they've rescued me from the hunters.'

Tilly looked round and saw that the mole-rats were standing in a line staring at her, nibbling rapidly as though they'd got things stuck between their teeth, and whispering to each other. She was worried. The guard had told her that they didn't like lizards much. What would they do to her?

They lowered their blunt flat heads like battering rams and moved slowly towards her.

Her heart started to thump in her throat. 'Hello,' she said, and she noticed how her voice had stopped being crackly and was suddenly squeaky with nerves. 'I'm Tilly Mint really.'

The largest mole-rat, who was pure white with big red eyes and fine quivering whiskers, stepped out of the line and came up to Tilly Mint, sniffing right up to her face. At last she stepped back, as if she was satisfied. 'Hello, Tilly Mint,' she said, and her voice was soft and silky, like a cat purring. 'I'm the queen of the mole-rats, and I'm very happy that you've come to visit us.'

She nodded to the others. Tilly suddenly found herself surrounded by mole-rats all sniffing round her so that they tickled her with their whiskers, and one or two of them began to lick her with quick, busy jabs of their tongue, making her want to giggle.

'Listen to me,' said the white queen of the mole-rats seriously. 'I am very pleased to meet you, Tilly Mint, because you seem to be a friend of the dodo bird's, and she's very special to us. But how did you get in? Usually only mole-rats and wounded animals in great danger can come down here. You smell of humans, and they're our greatest enemy. You also smell of lizards, and we don't like them much either. I can tell there's no danger about you . . . but how did you get past the guard?'

'He didn't want me to get past him!' said Tilly. 'He told me not to. But I had to find Dodo.'

The queen sniffed at Tilly again, then padded round her, deep in thought.

'Then how did you get past him?'

'It wasn't his fault,' said Tilly. 'Really it wasn't. You mustn't blame him. He didn't see me go past him.'

The queen swung round and padded round Tilly in the opposite direction. It made Tilly dizzy to watch her. 'He didn't see you!' She stopped and faced Tilly. 'This is very serious. Tell me. If he didn't see you . . . was it because he had his eyes closed?'

'Yes,' whispered Tilly.

'Was he singing, Tilly Mint?'

'Yes.'

The queen stopped. 'I thought so! I thought so!' she shouted. 'He must be punished!'

75

'No!' cried Tilly. 'Please don't punish him! It was my fault. I asked him to sing.'

The queen wasn't listening to her. She ran to two young mole-rats. 'You!' she said. 'Go to the entrance and fetch the guard to me. And you! Take his place at the entrance to our burrow. And remember . . . Never close your eyes! Never sing on duty! Let no stranger pass!' The two mole-rats scampered off out of the lit cavern into the darkness of the burrow.

The queen sighed. 'It is a very serious matter,' she told Tilly. 'Every second of our lives we must watch out for danger. The only peace we can hope to have is when we're here, resting in our cavern. What hope for us is there if our guard lets strangers through? Do you understand, Tilly Mint? This is the great hall of the mole-rats. Here are young mole-rats who are learning to hunt and dig and help us all to survive. And here are old mole-rats, who've spent their lives in service to the pack, and who deserve to rest peacefully, out of harm's way. And here are mother mole-rats, nursing their young. See the babies, Tilly Mint?'

In the quiet corners of the great hall Tilly could see mothers bent over little pink bundles, and she could hear the tiny squeaks of the babies as they opened up their mouths for food.

'Now do you understand, Tilly Mint? I must make sure that they're protected. I must! I must!'

Tilly nodded. Behind her, Dodo sniffed into her feathers. 'Nobody's safe!' she said.

'No,' agreed the mole-rat queen. 'Not when man's around. There's danger everywhere.'

They could hear a scampering down the tunnel that led to the great hall, and then behind it a slow dragging sound, like someone limping, and soon into the light the young mole-rat ran, and behind him limped the guard, his head bent, his whiskers trailing in the dust, all the song and the jigging gone from him.

'Come here, Guard,' said the white queen sternly. Slowly the guard walked over to her. 'I'm sorry, Queen,' he said hoarsely. He bowed his head.

'Sorry!' The queen shouted. 'Sorry!' Her voice echoed in the great hall, and fled tumbling down all the dark tunnels that led off from it.

Tilly turned away and buried her head in Dodo's side. She couldn't bear to look. 'Don't hurt him!' she begged. 'Don't hurt him.'

Then she realised that the queen was talking to the guard again, but softly, soft as a cat, kind and sad and gentle.

'You have failed us, Old Guard,' she said to him. 'We could have been killed in our merry-making. Remember the time the hunters came with dogs? Do you remember that time, Old Guard?'

77

'Yes, Queen.'

Tilly could hardly hear him.

'Tell us what happened, Old Guard, in case any of us has forgotten. I was only a mole-ratling then. But you remember, Guard. What happened?'

The older mole-rats huddled together and moaned, remembering terrible things. But the younger ones scampered up to the guard and gathered round him, wanting a story. The mothers hushed their whimpering babies so they could listen.

'It was four or five summers ago,' said the old guard. His voice was heavy and sad, as if he was telling a story that should never be forgotten. 'Some hunters came to the island with dogs and guns. They shot many of our fine animals. They put many in cages to take away in boats to distant lands. All the creatures hid where they could, terrified for their lives, too frightened to go out for food.

We mole-rats came in our hundreds to this great hall and cowered down in the darkness here. We didn't dare let the insects light it up for us even. We lay in the darkness for days and days, listening, listening out for danger. We had a guard at every entrance, and all the strong mole-rats were ready to rush out and defend the pack as soon as they got word of danger. Not a sound down here, for nights on end.

And then, one night, a dog broke through and came sneaking down one of the tunnel entrances without any of us hearing him. As soon as he got to the great hall he leapt on us with a howling and a lashing of his legs and a terrible clashing together of his great yellow teeth. He killed the queen . . .'

'I know,' the queen nodded. 'My grandmother. He killed my grandmother . . .'

'And he sent all the mole-rats fleeing for their lives down the tunnels, fleeing in every direction, and outside all the entrances men were waiting with guns to shoot us as we came out . . .'

'And many of our brothers and sisters were killed that day,' put in one of the very old mole-rats. 'I was a baby, clinging on to my mother's back. She was killed.'

'Many, many were killed.' The queen nodded. Her voice was very quiet in the tunnel. 'You've remembered it well, Old Guard. And can you remember one last thing? Can you remember how the hunter's dog got past the guard?'

It was a long time before the guard spoke again. He cleared his throat. 'Yes, Queen, I can remember,' he said. 'The guard was asleep.'

'Exactly,' said the queen. 'The guard was asleep. He had his eyes closed.'

In the silence that followed, Tilly crept away from Dodo and went over to the old guard. She

79

put her arms round his neck. 'I can see that Guard must be punished,' she said. 'But if you punish him, you must punish me as well, because I had to get past him to find Dodo. I'd have found a way somehow.'

'Oh dear,' said Dodo. 'Then I suppose it's all my fault for fainting. And it's the grey bird's fault for putting me in the tree. And it's the hunter's fault for coming here in the first place.'

'Yes!' chorused the old mole-rats, who'd grown up with the guard and who'd always been his friends, and jigged to his tunes as well, on their way down the tunnels. 'It's the hunter's fault. Blame the hunter!'

'Quiet!' shouted the queen. All the squeaks and shouts stopped. 'I must think about his punishment. Quiet!'

For a long time the queen paced the floor of the cavern while the waiting mole-rats shuffled and coughed and the babies murmured in their sleep. At last the queen stopped. Everyone's eyes were on her.

'His punishment,' she announced. 'Is that he will never, never, be allowed to guard the mole-rats again.'

Everyone nodded, even the old guard, at the justice of this punishment. He shuffled round to the back of the old mole-rats and stood there, head hung low, ashamed.

'And what about his reward?' demanded Dodo.

'Reward?' said the queen. 'How can I reward him for what he did?'

'He helped Tilly to find me again.'

'And he's got a lovely singing voice,' said Tilly. 'He ought to be rewarded for having such a nice voice. And he sang me a very important song.'

'Sing it!' demanded the queen.

So the old mole-rat guard shuffled forward again, and a bit timidly at first, and then growing more confident, he sang the song he'd sung at the entrance to the tunnel. His voice was pure and sweet, even for such an old mole-rat, and all the other mole-rats sang softly behind him, and the queen swayed backwards and forwards, and so did Dodo, still on her back.

'Beautiful!' They all said, when the old guard had shuffled back behind the line again.

'Your reward,' said the queen, purring again, 'is to take on the important and dangerous task of escorting Tilly Mint and Dodo out through the tunnels and back to daylight, where they belong.'

The old guard hobbled forward joyfully. 'With pleasure, Queen. Queen of the Night. White Lady of the Shadows. Moon of the Darknesses . . .'

'Now, now,' she purred. 'Don't get carried away. Take great care of them, old friend. Tilly Mint is a special visitor from England. Look after her. And Dodo . . .' She looked at Dodo, who was

81

struggling to turn round on to her stomach, with the help of Tilly and some of the stronger mole-rats, ' . . . Dodo is the most precious creature on the island. She may be the last of her kind. Take care! Take great care!'

Dodo was at last sorted out, and with a lot of fussing and squawking on her part and shouts and shoves from everyone else, she was pushed out of the great hall and into a tunnel that broadened out and up so that she could at least crawl.

'Goodbye, Queen Mole-rat,' said Tilly. 'Thank you very much for your help.'

'Goodbye, Tilly Mint.' The queen sniffed her so closely that her damp nose touched Tilly's cheek, and her quivering whiskers brushed her face. 'There is great danger ahead of you,' she whispered. 'But there's nothing more we can do to help you. Beware of the pirates, Tilly Mint! Beware! Beware!'

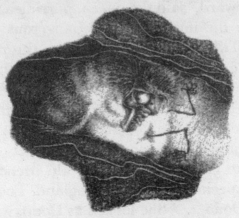

She stood back and Tilly ran to catch up with Dodo and Mole-rat. 'Goodbye, Tilly Mint!' all the little mole-rats called, jigging along the tunnel behind them as far as they dared. 'Goodbye Dodo.'

'Goodbye!' Dodo called gaily. 'Tilly, I can't tell you how good it is to be on my feet again! And we're off to the sunshine! Hooray!'

Old Mole-rat started to sing one of his jigging songs, and Dodo skipped happily behind him, knocking her head now and then on low bits of the tunnel, and tripping over Mole-rat's tail, and behind them ran Tilly, with the Queen Mole-rat's warning ringing in her head.

'Beware of the pirates, Tilly Mint! Beware! Beware!'

EIGHT

Beware of the Pirates

It was a long time before they began to see daylight. For hours they seemed to twist and twine through dark, damp tunnels, and though Mole-rat never stopped singing his voice began to grow weak and hoarse, and he stopped jigging and took up his dragging limp again. Dodo gave up trying to skip, and Tilly trailed a long way behind.

'I don't like it here much,' she said. 'I don't like the darkness.'

That started poor old tired Mole-rat singing his favourite song again:

'All things begin in darkness
In shell, in nut, in hole,
In seed, in spawn, in nest, in soil . . .'

and it was then that Tilly began to make out the beginning of daylight. It came like a tiny pinprick far away, and then it was like an eye, then a moon, and then the light came bursting through, flooding

84

the tunnel as if it was water rushing through it. The roof of the tunnel grew higher and higher, yet Tilly found she was having to stoop as she ran, and she realised that she could see her own Tilly Mint feet again in their stripy socks and pumps. She was well over the heads of Dodo and Mole-rat.

At last they were out of the tunnel. They seemed to be standing in a cave, and outside it they could hear the shush of the sea.

Dodo staggered against Tilly, exhausted. 'Phew!' she laughed. 'That was fun! Aren't we having fun these days, Tilly Mint!'

Mole-rat looked up at Tilly. 'You've grown a bit,' he said anxiously. 'You look a bit like a human now.'

'I am a human,' said Tilly. 'I'm a little girl.'

'She doesn't act like one though,' Dodo promised him. 'She acts more like a mole-rat.'

Tilly ran out of the cave onto the yellow sands of a little beach. 'Look at this!' she shouted. 'I'm going to paddle!' She kicked off her shoes and socks and waded into the blue-green water, and it lapped round her ankles as if it was trying to lick life back into her tired feet.

'Just the job!' shouted Mole-rat, and plunged in after her, paddling madly with all four feet at once. 'Haven't swum since I was a ratling!' He bobbed down and flicked over, waving his stubby legs in the air, and bobbed back over again.

'Come on in, Dodo-my-duckling!' he shouted. 'Get those feathers wet!'

Dodo shook her head shyly. 'Can't swim,' she said.

'I'll splash you if you don't!' Mole-rat scampered out onto the sands and shook himself, spraying her like a fountain. She screeched and flapped her short wings at him.

'Stop it, now, stop it, Mole-rat,' she scolded. 'Act your age! Behave yourself!'

'I only want you to enjoy yourself, Dodo-of-my-dreams!' he said. 'Come and wash your corns! And watch out for jellyfish!'

He scurried back into the sea, splashing Tilly as he ran past her, and struck out across the little bay, gurgling as he went:

Proper little squelchy things
Blobs of slime
Pink and purple bubbles
Dancers in the brine
Swirling out their skirtses
Watch them do their curtsies
Swaying in the waves like washing on the line . . .'

Tilly started after him. 'I know that song!' she shouted.

'Sing it then, Tilly-Winkle!' he called back to her, but she gazed after his little splashing head, trying to remember where she'd heard the song before, and who had sung it to her.

Meanwhile Dodo had stepped carefully onto a large knobbly stone that was just at the water's edge, and sat there preening herself. She splayed out her stumpy wings, shaking the dust off her feathers, and pecked them smooth again.

'Everything's all right now, isn't it Tilly?' she said.

'Yes,' said Tilly. 'It seems to be.' She lay on her back in the warm, kind water, and looked up at the blue sky with gulls wheeling over her head. It did seem then, that everything was all right again. The water rocked her gently.

Suddenly Dodo shrieked: 'Help me! Help me! I've been kidnapped!'

Tilly sat up in the water. Dodo had gone! She ran out on to the shore.

'Not that way!' Dodo squawked. 'Out here! Out here!'

Tilly turned round and saw Dodo flapping on her stone, which was briskly walking out to sea.

'I didn't know stones could swim!' wailed Dodo, as the stone lifted up its leathery flippers and floated off.

'I'm not a stone, I'm a turtle,' said the turtle. 'Can't sit about sunbathing all day just because I've got a bird on my back. You should look where you're sitting, gurgle-gurgle-gloop.' And with that

he dived down and disappeared under the water, and so did Dodo.

For a moment her head popped out again. 'Help! Drowning Dodo!' she bubbled, and was about to go under again when Mole-rat and Tilly splashed out to her and carried her back to shore. They tipped her onto the sand.

'What a mess I am now!' she moaned. 'Just look at my soggy feathers! And I'd just got them looking nice again after being dragged through all those tunnels.'

'Never mind, Dodo. You'll soon dry off. Lie down in the sand with Mole-rat and let the sun dry you.'

'I don't suppose there's anything to eat round here, is there?' Mole-rat sniffed the sand. 'I've left all my food behind.'

'What do you eat, Mole-rat?' asked Tilly.

'Bulbs and roots and things, deep in the soil,' Mole-rat sighed, dribbling a bit with hungry memories. 'And lovely juicy worms.'

'I'll see what I can find,' Tilly promised him. 'But you stay here and watch Dodo, won't you? She looks tired out after all that excitement.'

She clambered up a steep bank that led out of the little cove where Mole-rat and Dodo had stretched themselves out to sleep. 'Don't go away from there, will you?' she called to them. Dodo flapped her wing at her and waved her on her way.

Tilly went further and further into the jungle in her search for food. She was very hungry herself. She had no idea what a dodo might eat. The trees were heavy with all sorts of fruit, and as she reached up to pick some, Tilly saw a flying-squirrel leap off one high branch onto another tree.

'Wheee!' It shouted. 'Wheeeee!' Another one cast off after it. 'Wheeeeeeeee!'

They perched together on a branch and looked out across to the little cove where Tilly had been. More and more of them clustered on the branch, pointing to something far out to sea. They seemed to be saying something urgent to each other, and what they said came down like a whisper in the air, and seemed to be taken up again and floated off by humming insects, and drifted down again and whistled softly by slow-flying birds.

The further Tilly went into the bushes the greater the fluttering and whispering grew, till it seemed that the air of the island was buzzing with the same sad song: 'All the poor dodos . . . all the poor dodos . . . all the poor dodos . . .'

'What do you mean?' Tilly shouted. 'What's happening?'

A blue-green bird with golden eyes and a voice like a bell flew down and fluttered its wings rapidly so it hovered just over Tilly's head.

'Danger around. Danger everywhere,' it chimed. 'Pirate ship sailing. Beware. Beware . . .'

'A pirate ship!' Tilly dropped all the fruit she'd been gathering.

'Get back to her!' the chiming bird urged. 'Back to her!'

Tilly ran back to the cove, pushing her way through the trailing bushes, her breath throbbing in her throat. Far out on the horizon she could see the riggings of a tall sailing ship. But when she came to the edge of the little bay she could only stand, helpless, staring at the place where Dodo and the mole-rat had been lying.

Because both of them had gone.

NINE

The World Belongs to All of Us

Dodo had been the first to go. As soon as Tilly had gone in search of food she opened her eyes and stretched herself. 'Mole-rat,' she said.

He snored and turned over.

'Mole-rat. Have all the dodos really gone?'

He snored again, rubbing his paw across his eye-lid as a fly balanced there.

'I have to know,' said Dodo. 'I have to know if it's really true.' Her voice was low and clucking. She pecked his head to try and wake him up. He tucked his paws round his ears.

'Then I'm going to find out for myself,' she said.

She took a run at the bank, wishing she could just spread out her wings and fly up it like any normal bird. The sand was soft and deep, and she kept sliding down again, but at last she made it to the top. With her last little flurry the fine sand sprayed behind her and showered like drizzle into Mole-rat's open mouth.

He jumped to his feet and looked round,

blinking, not knowing at first what had woken him up, and then with a terrible panicky dawning of dread he realised that he had been asleep, and that he'd lost Dodo.

'Dodo! Dodo!' he wailed. He ran frantically in larger and larger circles. His long life underground had given him very poor eyesight; he could only really follow smells, or very clear tracks when they were right under his nose. But the sand was all scuffed up, and the smells were everywhere. He could just trace his own pawmarks, and then the marks left by Tilly's shoes, and at last, just when he'd given up hope and knew he'd have to go back down the tunnel for the queen's punishment, he found clawmarks in the bank.

He lunged up the hill, crazy with guilt. Dodo's tracks led him into the jungle, and then, as the undergrowth grew thicker, they disappeared. 'Now what? Now what?' he shouted. His whiskers quivered. 'I'm a stupid old mole-rat. I should never have been allowed to look after Dodo. I'm not fit to be given a job like that.' He rushed into the foliage, sniffing for any scent that might help him. 'Think! Think, you old fool,' he told himself. He splayed his legs out and sank down, and almost immediately jumped up again. 'The dodo's nesting-place!' he shouted. 'That's where she'll be.'

And that was where he found her, sitting with

her head down and her beak tucked into her wing. Around her were scattered a few twigs and sticks, all that remained of the dodos' nests. Tiny fragments of eggshell glinted in the earth.

Dodo didn't look up when he tiptoed over to her.

'You won't find any dodos nesting here,' he said to her gently. 'They've all gone, Dodo. Really. They've all been killed.'

She was making a low, brooding, froofy sound in her throat. 'I had to find out for myself, Mole-rat. Just to make sure.'

He nodded. 'I know. Come on now. We'll have to get back to Tilly. She'll be terribly worried, you know.'

Tilly stood at the top of the bank, gazing down at the place where she'd last seen Dodo and Mole-rat.

'I'll never see them again,' she thought. She felt a feather tickling her leg, and realised that they were standing right next to her.

'Where've you been?' she shouted.

'Oh, nowhere,' said Dodo. 'I wanted to go for a little walk, and, naturally, Mole-rat came too.'

'I was worried about you, Dodo,' said Tilly, crouching down to her. 'I thought something was after you.'

'There's usually something after me,' Dodo agreed. 'I'm very popular.'

'Don't be silly, Dodo.' Tilly wasn't in the mood

for laughing at Dodo now. 'Why can't they leave you alone?'

'I don't think they ever will, Tilly.' Dodo tried to comfort her.

'Then it's not fair,' said Tilly. 'It's just not fair. The world belongs to all of us.'

'The great of us, and the small of us,' Dodo agreed sadly. 'But some people just don't seem to want to share it.'

'But it's your world too,' Tilly said.

'I know,' Dodo nodded. 'And I like being here.' She patted Tilly's hand with her wing. 'One day,' she said. 'One day, people might understand that.'

And it seemed to Tilly then that Dodo wasn't a funny, stupid bird any more, or that she ever had been really, but that she was trying hard to shake away a real, deep sadness that only hunted animals know about.

'Tilly,' said Dodo. 'I want you to listen very carefully. I've got a present for you. It's a very special present. I want to give it to you very soon, and I want you to take it back home with you . . .'

'What do you mean?' asked Tilly. She felt suddenly sick with dread.

'Just listen, Tilly. I want you to take it home, all the way back home to England, and I want you to show it to all the children there. And to all the people who love animals. Oh, and birds, and fishes, and flowers, and trees. All the people who want to share their world with them. Will you do that?'

'Of course I will, Dodo. But I don't understand . . . I'm not going without you, Dodo. I'm not. I'm not!'

'I think you may have to.' Dodo turned away. 'I'll go and fetch it now.' And she waddled away into the trees again.

'Dodo! Come back!' Tilly shouted.

'It's all right Tilly, I'll watch her. She'll be quite safe in the jungle,' Mole-rat promised. He twitched his nose up, as if he was sniffing for danger. 'This is where she must be careful, by the shore. You keep guard here. This is where you're needed.'

'Mole-rat! What do you mean?' asked Tilly, but Mole-rat only sighed, and shook his head, and cleared his throat a few times. 'Don't set me off, Tilly,' he said sadly. 'You know what I'm like.'

'But where's she gone now?'

'She's gone to a little clearing. A nesting-place. It's just up there. It's where . . . where . . .' He coughed and cleared his throat again. 'Where the dodos used to lay their eggs. Only not now. Not now. None left, you see.'

Tilly stared after her. 'Go with her, Mole-rat,' she begged. 'Guard her. Please.'

And Mole-rat scrabbled up the sandy bank and followed Dodo back into the jungle.

Tilly sat down wearily. It would be lovely to go to sleep, she thought. To go back home and sleep. It was very warm on the beach, and the sound of the waves lapping on the sand was soothing and gentle. She closed her eyes to listen to it. But she must keep guard. She must!

Suddenly she heard the sound of voices across the water, sharp, heavy men's voices, and she opened her eyes to see that it was beginning to grow cool and dark, and that there was a rowing boat pulling in to shore. Two men climbed out, one tall and one short; one old and one young.

They hauled their boat onto the sand. One of the men held up a spyglass to his eye and peered round the island with it.

As soon as she saw their swarthy faces and rich clothing Tilly knew who they were. They were pirates. Never, never, had she felt so afraid.

TEN

The Song of the Dodo

The two men heaved their boat up onto the shore. It rasped like sandpaper rubbing on stone. When they stood up Tilly could see that the tallest one had a long, tufty black beard. He strode across the sand in an angry mood. The younger one, a lad, had to run to keep up with him. Tilly crouched down and crept backwards towards the cave. 'Keep away, Dodo,' she thought. 'Keep away!'

Blackbeard began to shout angrily over his shoulder. 'What Godforsaken land is this, brother? I'm hungry!'

'Have some fish!' snarled Pirate Lad, handing him a raw steak of fish with a bite taken out of it. Blackbeard slapped it out of his hand.

'I think not, brother. I've had enough of that stuff.'

Tilly peered out at them from the shelter of the cave, hardly daring to breathe.

Pirate Lad stopped and sniffed, turning his head from side to side. He beckoned to

Blackbeard. 'D'you smell what I smell, brother? There's dodo in the air!'

'Oh no!' gasped Tilly.

He dropped down onto his knees to examine the sand. 'And look at this! Dodo tracks!'

Blackbeard leaned down over him, and nodded slowly.

'What wouldn't I give, brother, for a dish of dodo stew! Swimming in gravy!'

Pirate Lad stood up and spat into the sand.

'Dodo stew's like vomit, brother!'

Blackbeard thrust his face close up to Pirate Lad's, his beard like a bristly brush scratching his cheek. They looked angry enough to fight each other.

'Best food on earth, is dodo . . .' he argued, and, very faint, very far away, almost as if it was in Tilly's own head, came the sound of Dodo's voice: 'Oh, thank you, Sir! Thank you!'

'Stay there, Dodo,' groaned Tilly. 'Stay there, please!' The two pirates were standing stock still, straining to listen to the distant sound through all the stirrings of the jungle.

Then the first pirate said softly:

'What sound would you say that was, brother? I haven't heard that sound in months . . . but I'd bet you a purse of guineas that it's the cry of the dodo bird.'

'How can it be!' Pirate Lad scoffed. 'There's no

dodos left. You've ate 'em all, I bet! They're all dead now, brother. They're extinct.'

And again, as tiny as if it was only in her head, Tilly heard Dodo's voice. 'They don't stink.'

Completely forgetting her own fear of the pirates, Tilly stood up and shouted as hard as she could.

'Run, Dodo! Run! Run for your life!' And as she said that the beasts and the birds of the island sent up their clamour, a deafening roar like mountains breaking open. They flapped their wings and leapt into bushes and crashed through trees, all to hide the sound of Dodo coming back towards the shore, and to cover up the sight of her yellow feathers in the dusk.

'Go away, Dodo!' Tilly screamed, and all the creatures screamed it with her. 'Run!'

Tilly started to run up the fine sand at the side of the bank that would take her up to Dodo. Blackbeard grabbed her and hauled her back down again. The pirates stood each side of her, and hissed at her, one down each ear, as if they were singing her a terrible mocking song.

'You know where that bird is!'

'You're hiding it from us!'

'She's the only one left! Leave her! Leave her alone!' Tilly begged.

'Then tell us where to find it –'

'Or we'll spoil your face!'

'No!' shouted Tilly. 'She's the only dodo in the world!'

'I'm here,' came Dodo's voice, calm and quiet behind them.

All the crying and clamour of the creatures died away to nothing. The pirates froze, with their arms held up to strike, like statues. Day had drained away into moonlight.

Dodo stepped forward. She held an egg in her folded wings, and she nodded to Tilly to come and take it from her. And in a voice that was as soft as a whisper, Dodo sang her the only song she knew; the song of the last dodo.

This is the egg
The golden egg
The special egg from long ago
Take it back to England
For children there to know.

For children who love animals
In air, on earth, in sea,
Who keep the forest places
For creatures to roam free
For children who let flowers grow,
And butterfly, and bee,

Who leave the fishes in their stream
And leave the spiders on their web
And leave the birds' eggs in their nest
And leave the beetle on its log.

This lovely, living planet
Belongs to every thing
That moves and breathes upon it;
A song of life I sing.

So take this egg
This golden egg
This special egg from long ago

And keep it safe
In memory
Of the life
And death
Of the last dodo.'

ELEVEN

In Memory

Tilly knew then that this was the last time she would ever see Dodo.

She tried to rush forward to hug her again but all the jungle creatures closed in a ring round Dodo and the pirates, keeping Tilly back so she couldn't see what was happening.

All the mole-rats came up from their burrows, led by their red-eyed queen. The lizards slid out from under rocks and stones, and the snakes slithered through the grass. Monkeys swung across the branches, and flying-squirrels leapt into the air after them, and grey hooded birds swooped down, and red fire-birds, and insects with starlight on their wings, and all kinds of creatures that Tilly had never seen before, all clustering round Dodo and the pirates, all bowing their heads in silence.

For that was a terrible day, when the last of the dodos was killed by pirates, and it really happened, a long time ago.

And when the animals moved away the pirates

had gone, and so had Dodo. All that was left of her was a handful of yellow feathers on the ground, swirling in the evening wind, and a sudden gust took them up and up, away over the trees, away over the island, into the floating path of the moon, so that for a second they looked like a yellow-grey bird in flight.

'Goodbye, Dodo,' Tilly called.

And then they were gone.

But Tilly could hear the splash of oars on the dark sea, and the cruel laughter of the pirate brothers as they rowed back to their ship. Far out on the horizon she could see the pirate ship moored, with little lanterns swinging on it. She could hear the voices of men drifting across the water.

All the stars in the sky were reflected in the black, deep sea, and they were like the eyes of animals, cold and angry. Tilly was alone, and night was falling fast, fast all around her.

'I want to go home!' said Tilly. 'Home! Home! I want to go home.'

Then the wind of the night came rushing up to her, and lifted her as if she had no weight at all, and carried her like a leaf, or a balloon, or a bird's feather, or a speck of dream-dust. Voices kept coming to her, in and out of her mind:

'Best food on earth is dodo.'

'Wait till I catch the dodo!'

107

'The world belongs to all of us.'

'All the poor dodos.'

'Dodos are like dinosaurs, they're all dead now' . . . over and over again in her mind, and then one voice kept coming through, stronger than the others, and closer than them . . .

'It's no good crying over dead dodos. Crying won't bring them back.' She knew that voice.

'Mrs Hardcastle! Mrs Hardcastle!' she called.

Now she could see right down through treetops. She could see the surprised face of a badger peering up at her, and a hedgehog snuffling through leaves. She could see a mouse stretching out its back legs, and a rabbit nibbling lettuce leaves. Day was just starting. She was looking down inside the biggest tree in the forest, a huge chestnut tree with white flowers like Christmas tree candles on its branches. And there was Mrs Hardcastle, yawning and rubbing her eyes as if she was just waking up from a sleep.

'Mrs Hardcastle, Mrs Hardcastle!' Tilly could hear her own voice, far away as if it was in a dream. 'Oh, Mrs Hardcastle! I want to tell you . . . the island, and the big hunters . . . and the pirates came . . . oh . . . and the dodo, Mrs Hardcastle. The dodo. Did it really, really happen?'

And though she was whirling round so fast now that she couldn't see Mrs Hardcastle any more, she could hear her voice, as close to her ear as if she was up in the sky next to her . . .

'Yes, it all really happened Tilly. A long, long time ago. Tell the children, Tilly Mint. Tell the children . . . Captain Cloud will help you . . .'

And Mrs Hardcastle's voice grew fainter and fainter, and the whirl of the wind tossed Tilly gently till she felt as if she was being rocked in a little boat on a lapping stream, and she could hear the sound of someone singing about jellyfish . . .

'Proper little squelchy things
Blobs of slime
Pink and purple bubbles,
Like dancers in the brine . . .'

and she knew that any minute now the rocking would stop and she would come up with a bump against the wall of Captain Cloud's boatshed.

The jolt made her open her eyes. It was her bedroom door being opened. She was lying in bed, with Mr Pig tucked under the pillow and the sun warm on her through her window.

'Awake at last!' Mum laughed. She sat on Tilly's bed. 'What a night it's been, Tilly! All that wind! And you didn't sleep very well, did you? I heard you shouting out for Mrs Hardcastle.'

Tilly stared out of the window. She was sure . . . sure . . .

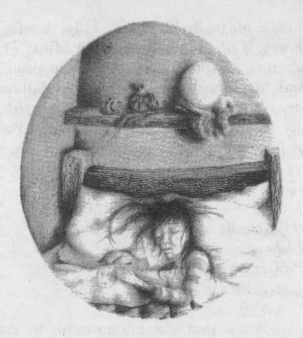

'Tilly,' said Mum gently. 'Mrs Hardcastle isn't going to come back again. You know that, don't you?'

Tilly nodded.

'I went round to her house last night,' Mum said. 'I wanted to help her brother to clear out her attic. And we found something that we thought you'd like to keep. You were fast asleep when I brought it in, Tilly. So I put it there for you. Look. On your special shelf.'

'The egg! It's my egg!' Tilly gasped. She jumped out of her bed and ran to her shelf. She kept all kinds of special things there, like a conker, and a blue feather, and a bag full of sparkling dream-dust. And in the middle now was an egg, big as a golden melon, and yellow with age. She picked it up carefully.

'Captain Cloud thought you'd like it,' said Mum. 'I don't know what it is though. Do you?'

'Yes,' said Tilly. 'It's a special egg. A magic egg from long ago.'

She put it back, very carefully, on her shelf.

'I'll keep it safe
In memory
Of the life
And death
Of the last dodo.'

'Mum,' she said. 'I want to tell all the children about the dodo. D'you think Captain Cloud would help me?'

'I'm sure he would,' said Mum.

After breakfast Tilly went to Captain Cloud's house, and she told him the story of the last of the dodos.

'That's a very important story, Tilly Lizard,' he told her when she'd finished. He stroked his beard thoughtfully. 'I'll tell you what. I'll fetch you some paper and a pencil, and we'll make it into a book, shall we?'

111 .

And this is it:

It was a very windy night; the sort of night that sounds as if wild animals are roaring round the houses and pawing at the door to be let in